This book belongs to

. . . .

Front endpapers by Johannes Vogenauer aged 10 (left) and Katia Blin aged 5 (right)
Back endpapers by Ka Keung Tsang aged 9 (left) and Anushka Chaudhury aged 8 (right)
Thank you to St Barnabas Primary School, Oxford for helping with the endpapers – K.P.

OXFORD
UNIVERSITY PRESS

Great Clarendon Street, Oxford OX2 6DP

Oxford University Press is a department of the University of Oxford.
It furthers the University's objective of excellence in research, scholarship,
and education by publishing worldwide in

Oxford New York

Auckland Cape Town Dar es Salaam Hong Kong Karachi
Kuala Lumpur Madrid Melbourne Mexico City Nairobi
New Delhi Shanghai Taipei Toronto

With offices in
Argentina Austria Brazil Chile Czech Republic France Greece
Guatemala Hungary Italy Japan Poland Portugal Singapore
South Korea Switzerland Thailand Turkey Ukraine Vietnam

First published 1987
This 25th anniversary edition published in 2012

British Library Cataloguing in Publication Data
Data available

ISBN: 978-0-19-279305-8 (paperback)
ISBN: 978-0-19-279306-5 (hardback)
ISBN: 978-0-19-279307-2 (paperback with audio CD)

1 3 5 7 9 10 8 6 4 2

Printed in China

Paper used in the production of this book is a natural, recyclable product made
from wood grown in sustainable forests. The manufacturing process conforms
to the environmental regulations of the country of origin

Valerie Thomas and Korky Paul

Winnie the Witch

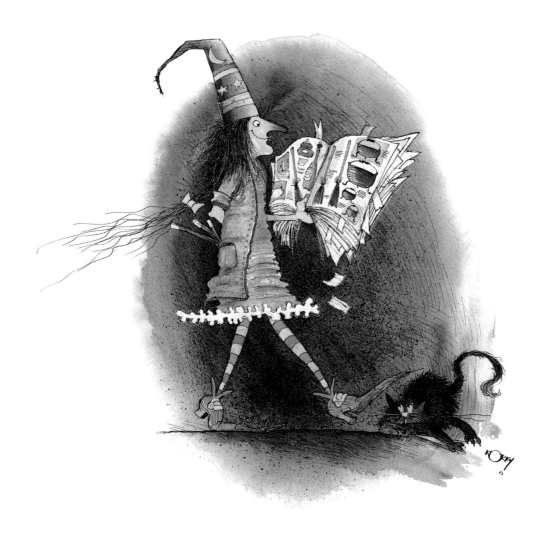

UNIVERSITY PRESS

Winnie the Witch lived in a black
house in the forest.
The house was black on the
outside and black on the inside.
The carpets were black.
The chairs were black.
The bed was black and it had
black sheets and black blankets.
Even the bath was black.

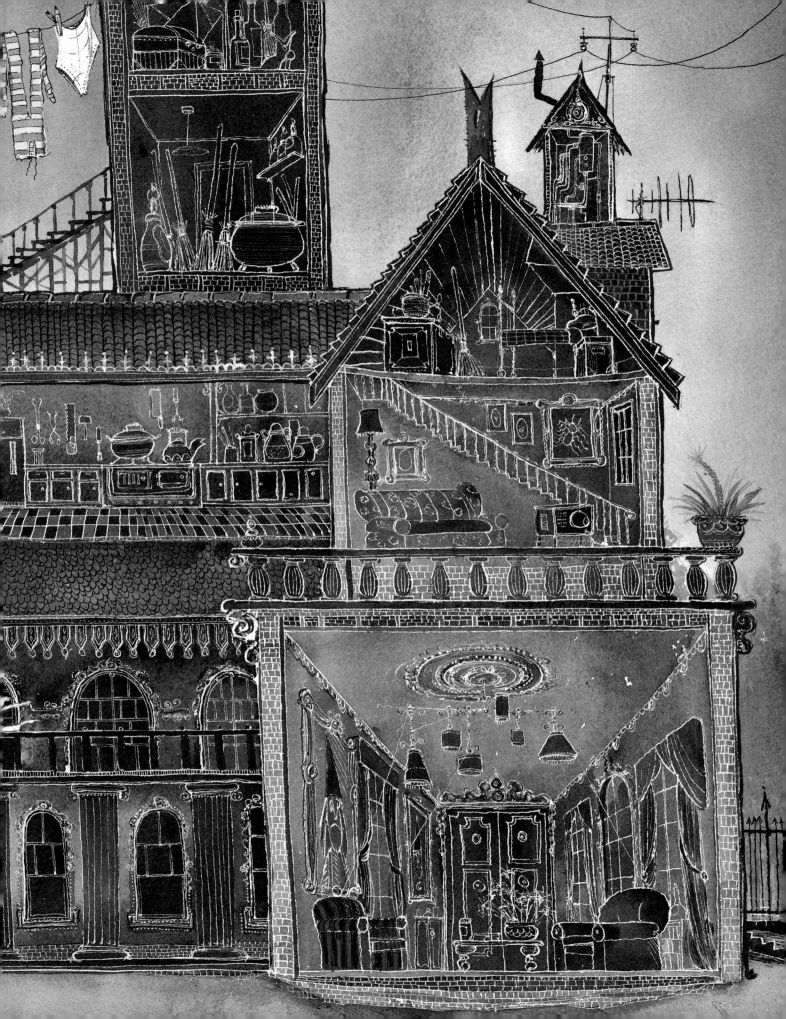

Winnie lived in her black house with her cat, Wilbur.
He was black too. And that is how the trouble began.

When Wilbur sat on a chair with
his eyes open, Winnie could see him.
She could see his eyes, anyway.

But when Wilbur closed his eyes
and went to sleep, Winnie couldn't
see him at all. So she sat on him.

When Wilbur sat on the carpet with his eyes open, Winnie could see him. She could see his eyes, anyway.

But when Wilbur closed his
eyes and went to sleep,
Winnie couldn't see him at all.
So she tripped over him.

One day, after a nasty fall, Winnie
decided something had to be done.
She picked up her magic wand,
waved it once and ABRACADABRA!
Wilbur was a black cat no longer.
He was bright green!

Abracadabra!

Now, when Wilbur slept on a chair, Winnie could see him.

When Wilbur slept on the floor, Winnie could see him.

And she could see him
when he slept on the bed.
But, Wilbur was not allowed
to sleep on the bed . . .

. . . so Winnie put
him outside.
Outside in
the grass.

Winnie came hurrying outside,
tripped over Wilbur,
turned three somersaults,
and fell into a rose bush.

When Wilbur sat outside in the grass,
Winnie couldn't see him, even when
his eyes were wide open.

This time, Winnie was furious.
She picked up her magic wand,
waved it five times and . . .

... **Abracadabra!** Wilbur had a red head, a yellow body, a pink tail, blue whiskers, and four purple legs. But his eyes were still green.

Now, Winnie could see Wilbur when he sat on a chair, when he lay on the carpet, when he crawled into the grass.

And even when
he climbed to
the top of the
tallest tree.

Wilbur climbed to the top of the tallest tree to hide.
He looked ridiculous and he knew it.
Even the birds laughed at him.

Wilbur was miserable.
He stayed at the top
of the tree all day
and all night.

Next morning Wilbur
was still up the tree.
Winnie was worried.
She loved Wilbur
and hated him to
be miserable.

Then Winnie had an idea.
She waved her magic wand
and *Abracadabra!*
Wilbur was a black cat once more.
He came down from the tree, purring.

Then Winnie waved her wand again, and again, and again.

Abracadabra!

Now instead of a black house, she had a yellow house with a red roof and a red door. The chairs were white with red and white cushions. The carpet was green with pink roses.

The bed was blue, with pink and white sheets and pink blankets. The bath was a gleaming white.

And now, Winnie can see Wilbur no matter where he sits.